Three Cheers for Hippo!

John Stadler

A Harper Trophy Book

Harper & Row, Publishers

Library of Congress Cataloging-in-Publication Data
Stadler, John.
  Three cheers for Hippo!

  Summary: Hippo cleverly comes up with a plan to
save Cat, Pig, and Dog just when it looks as if they are
about to parachute into a swamp full of alligators.
  [1. Animals—Fiction] I. Title.
PZ7.S77575Th 1987   [E]   87-497
ISBN 0-690-04668-5
ISBN 0-690-04670-7 (lib. bdg.)
ISBN 0-06-443220-3 (pbk.)

Published in hardcover by Thomas Y. Crowell, New York.
First Harper Trophy edition, 1990.

Hippo is here.

Cat speaks.

Hippo holds Cat's hand.

Hippo flies the plane.

Pig and Dog are happy.

Cat is scared.

They jump.

Cat wants help.

Hippo is near.

The chutes open.

They float down.

Cat has fun.

The swamp is below.

Cat wonders.

Gators!

Cat is upset.

The gators look up.

Hippo flies by.

The gators wait.

They are nervous.

There are many gators.

They worry.

The table is set.

They want Hippo.

The gators open wide.

The table shakes.

Hippo rises.

The gators run away.

Hippo is here.